Here he is!

He's all the way from planet Earth.

Imagine that!

That is his spaceship.
Oops!

Luckily, my Dad is a UFO expert
so he can fix it. Till then, the
alien is staying with me!

Mum said my alien had better have a wash and a spot of breakfast after his long journey . . .

but I don't think he likes slime baths . . .

or
Jupiter
jellyfish.

When we got to school, he REALLY didn't like the look of my teacher, Miss Eight-Eyes.

It was quite embarrassing at lunch time because my alien REFUSED to eat with his toes!

And after school, when I took him to the playground, he couldn't moonwalk OR solar surf.

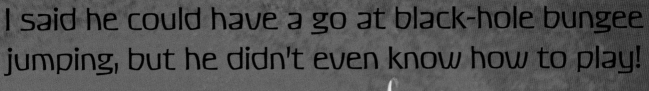
I said he could have a go at black-hole bungee jumping, but he didn't even know how to play!

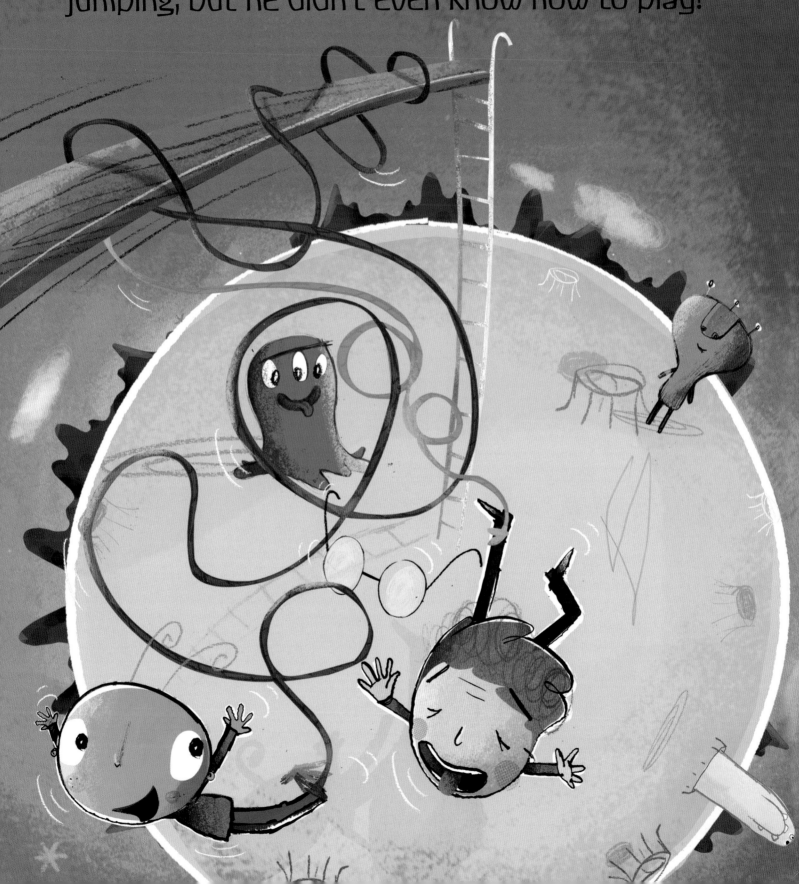

I don't want to look after my alien anymore.

My alien LOOKS strange.
He ACTS strange.

And he doesn't
know how to
play ANY
good games . . .

'I wish
you'd
go
home!'
I said.

A little tear rolled down my alien's cheek.

I checked
the
Crater Café . . .

and the
Lunar
Lighthouse . . .

and the
Asteroid Adventure
Playground, but
he wasn't
anywhere.

At last I spotted a
light in his spaceship . . .
Poor alien. I expect he's
wishing he could go home.

I went up to the door. I think my alien could tell
I was sorry. He invited me into his UFO . . .

and it was
AMAZING!

Since then I've been learning lots of
things about my alien and his planet.

He's taught
me about
funny
aliens
called
pirates ...

and
ferocious
aliens
called
dinosaurs.

He's even shown me how to play alien **rock guitar!**

My alien is enjoying some of our ways, too.

And he's become a solar surfing champion!

In fact, I'm not sure that aliens are really all that different from us after all.

They're just a bit uglier.

And some of us don't seem to think they're ugly at all.

We've been having lots of fun, my alien and me, but today Dad told us that the spaceship is fixed.

I don't want my alien to leave, but he has to go . . . He's got a mum and dad, too. He's even got an annoying little sister, like I do!

my FRIEND.

My friend has made me promise to write to him, but I'm going to do much better than that . . .

I'm planning a surprise visit!
I hope all the other aliens will be pleased to see me!